J

2

1

Get

Please
You can
Or by

D1080327

C032704161

Macbeth

Based on the play by
William Shakespeare

Retold by Conrad Mason

Illustrated by
Christa Unzner

Reading consultant: Alison Kelly
Roehampton University

Characters in the story

Macbeth

Lady Macbeth

Banquo

Macduff

Ross

Duncan, King of Scotland

Malcolm

Three witches

Contents

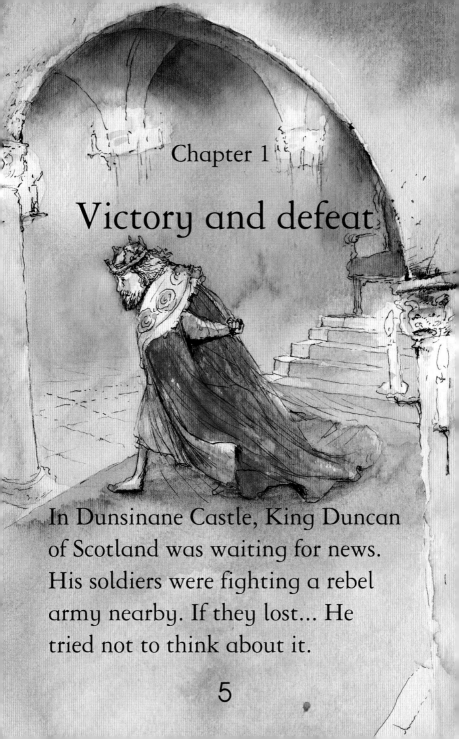

Chapter 1

Victory and defeat

In Dunsinane Castle, King Duncan of Scotland was waiting for news. His soldiers were fighting a rebel army nearby. If they lost... He tried not to think about it.

The doors to the throne room crashed open, and Duncan's son staggered in, supporting a wounded warrior.

"Father," Prince Malcolm panted, "this man has just come from the battlefield!"

"What news?" asked the king, nervously.

"Victory sire," the warrior gasped, "thanks to your general, Macbeth."

He killed the rebel leader.

King Duncan sighed with relief.

"Find the man a doctor," he ordered, as Malcolm helped the warrior out of the room.

Then Duncan called for his trusted advisor, Lord Ross. "Go to Macbeth," he said, "and tell him I shall reward him for his bravery."

Chapter 2

The witches

Meanwhile, Macbeth and his
friend Banquo were riding home
from the battlefield.

All at once, a mist sprang up,
swirling around them, and the sky
grew dark.

Macbeth pulled up his horse with
a yell of fright.

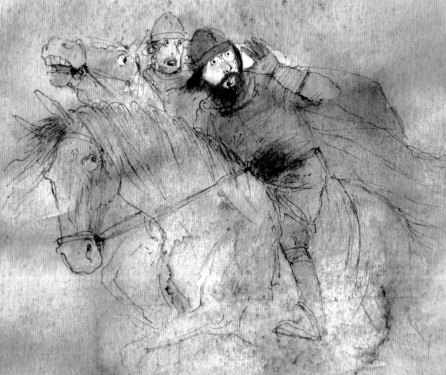

In front of them, three figures
loomed out of the mist.

10

They were old, ugly hags,
all dressed in black cloaks.

"Who are you?" cried Macbeth. He tried to sound brave, but inside he was terrified.

"Hail Macbeth, Lord of Cawdor, and future king of Scotland!" the hags cackled.

"Wait, what do you mean?"
demanded Banquo. "Who says
Macbeth is the Lord of Cawdor?"
But the figures had vanished.

Macbeth's eyes grew wide.
"Were they witches?" he whispered.

Before Banquo could reply, a horseman rode out of the mist. It was Lord Ross.

"Macbeth," he called. "I bring great news. King Duncan has made you Lord of Cawdor."

Banquo was amazed. "So they were right after all," he thought. He turned to look at his friend.

But Macbeth was gazing into the distance, lost in thought.

Chapter 3

Murderous plans

In the tallest tower of Inverness
Castle, Lady Macbeth was reading
a letter from her husband.

"Well, well, three witches said you'd be king!" she murmured. "But are you brave enough to make our dreams come true?"

As she pondered, the door opened and Macbeth came in.

Welcome home!

He threw his sword and helmet on the bed and hugged his wife.

She stepped back and looked into his eyes. "My husband," she said, "if you're to be King of Scotland, only one man stands in your way – and that's Duncan."

Macbeth shut his eyes. Ever since meeting the witches, he had been haunted by thoughts of killing Duncan. He wanted to be king, just as they had promised.

But the thought of murder filled him with dread.

"No," he said, turning away.

"You coward!" spat Lady Macbeth. "This is your chance to be king. Everyone knows you deserve it. What's more, Duncan is coming to visit this very night!"

20

Macbeth thought again. He couldn't do it – could he? The thought of a glittering crown filled his heart with excitement and greed.

Chapter 4

Death in the night

The great hall of Inverness Castle rang with music and laughter. At the end of the table, King Duncan chatted with Lady Macbeth.

Meanwhile, Macbeth stood alone in the moonlit courtyard. His mind was made up – Duncan would die. He just wished that it was over and done with.

Slowly, he walked back to the great hall, praying that the hours would pass more quickly.

At long last, Duncan and his lords went to bed, and the servants put out the torches. Silence filled the dark castle.

Macbeth took a deep breath, and wiped his brow. It was time.

But as he approached the steps
to Duncan's room, he stopped
dead. Was his mind playing tricks?
In the darkness he could see a
dagger, dripping with blood.

He shook his head. Nothing
there. Clutching his own dagger,
Macbeth climbed the steps...

The next morning, the castle woke to a terrible howl from Duncan's room.

"Murder! Murder!"

Everyone jumped out of bed and rushed to see what was happening.

Oh horror!

They soon found King Duncan – dead.

"Who did this?" thundered Macbeth. No one had an answer. Only Macbeth knew the truth, and he kept it to himself.

In silence, the lords stared at their dead king.

Chapter 5

To kill a friend

A week had passed. Macbeth sat alone in the great throne room at Dunsinane Castle, thinking.

After Duncan's murder, Prince Malcolm had gone missing, and the lords had crowned Macbeth instead. He was king!

Now he had everything he wanted. But he wasn't happy. He was thinking of Banquo. Banquo knew about the witches. What if he guessed who killed Duncan?

There was only one solution –
Banquo would have to die, too.
Macbeth rang for a servant.

You sent for me,
my lord?

"Listen closely," Macbeth told
him. "Tonight I am holding a feast
for all my lords. Find Banquo, and
make sure that he never arrives."

The servant bowed and left. Alone again, Macbeth thought of his best friend Banquo, who would soon be dead.

A sick feeling swept over him, made up of fear, sadness, and terrible, terrible guilt. His life was turning into a nightmare.

That night, two horsemen trotted
through a gloomy forest, on their
way to the feast. It was Banquo
and his son, Fleance.

Fleance shivered, and pulled his
cloak tighter around his shoulders.

"Looks like rain,"
grumbled Banquo.

"Let it pour," said a voice from
the bushes.

33

Before Banquo could react, he was on the ground, with someone's knee on his chest. Men stood all around, their daggers gleaming in the dark.

"Run!" Banquo howled at Fleance. The terrified boy turned his horse and sped off as fast as he could.

Banquo reached for his sword, but it was too far away. There was nothing he could do. He closed his eyes as the daggers came closer...

Chapter 6

The haunting

Macbeth's feast was nearly over
when something terrible happened.

He looked around at the happy
guests and smiled. Then he froze.
There, at the end of the table,
was Banquo.

Macbeth stumbled to his feet and
cried out in fear. At once, everyone
stopped talking.

"What's wrong, my dearest?"
asked Lady Macbeth.

"You should be dead!" croaked
Macbeth, pointing at Banquo.

The lords couldn't see
Banquo – just an empty place.

Banquo's face was deathly white, and his clothes were stained with blood. He glared at Macbeth, saying nothing.

"A ghost!" stammered Macbeth. "It wasn't me! I didn't kill you!" But the ghost had gone.

Murmurs ran around the table.

"Get out!" shouted Macbeth. "All of you. Leave me alone."

The puzzled lords stood and hurried out, casting worried glances at their king.

In minutes, only Macbeth and his wife were left. He turned to her, and saw that her eyes were filling with tears.

"Can we ever
forget what we've done?"
she wept.
Macbeth took her hand
and tried to comfort her,
but she wouldn't look at him.
Murder was driving them apart.

Chapter 7

Three prophecies

The wind howled across the moor, and rain fell in thick sheets.

"I need to speak to you, witches," called Macbeth. "Where are you?"

At once, they appeared.

"What's to become of me?"
Macbeth demanded.

"Fear Macduff,
the Lord of Fife,"
cried one.

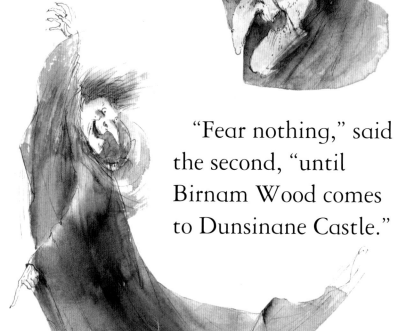

"Fear nothing," said
the second, "until
Birnam Wood comes
to Dunsinane Castle."

Macbeth sighed with relief.
"That can never happen," he
smiled. "I'm safe."

"Fear no man," said the third witch, "that was born of a woman."

"Then I really have nothing to fear," said Macbeth, laughing. "Every man was born of a woman – even Macduff."

The witches gave no reply. They
faded into the rain, and were gone.

"My lord?"
Macbeth turned to see a
messenger, waiting patiently with
his horse. "Yes?" he asked.

"Lord Macduff has found Prince Malcolm, in England," said the messenger. "He hopes to bring him back and make him king."

Macbeth went pale. "So be it!" he raged. "Macduff will pay for his treachery. Order my men to enter his castle, and kill his wife and children."

Chapter 8

The tide turns

In England, Prince Malcolm sat
with Lord Macduff beside a stream.
It was a beautiful day. Birds flew
overhead, and the sun shone.

"It's time for you to come back to
Scotland," said Macduff, gravely.
"You should be king. It was
Macbeth who killed your father
– I'm sure of it."

Malcolm said nothing. He was
deep in thought.

Then his face broke into a
smile. He had spotted Lord Ross
approaching across the meadow,
and he leaped up to greet him.

"Lord Ross, my father's friend!"
he cried.

But Ross didn't seem happy to see Malcolm.

"Lord Macduff, I have something dreadful to tell you," he said. "The tyrant Macbeth has killed your wife and children."

Macduff's face twisted with grief and fury. Then he spoke, his voice calm and cold. "Now you see why you must return," he said.

"Very well," said Malcolm. "Macbeth must be stopped. Tomorrow we march to Dunsinane."

Chapter 9

Macbeth's last stand

When news spread that Malcolm was on his way, the lords of Scotland flocked to join him. By now, everyone guessed that it was Macbeth who had killed Duncan.

At Birnam Wood, Malcolm halted his army. "Cut branches from the trees," he ordered. "We'll hide behind them when we attack Dunsinane Castle."

As the army advanced, hidden behind their shield of leaves, it seemed as if the great forest itself was moving.

From the battlements, Macbeth watched in panic. Just as the witches had promised, Birnam Wood was coming to Dunsinane.

A moment later, a horrible scream came from inside the castle, and a servant rushed out, his hands covered in blood. "My lord," he stammered, "it's your wife. She's killed herself."

Macbeth went white. He understood at once – guilt had driven his wife to this. He felt lonely, and numb with fear.

But there was no time to grieve. "Bring me my sword," he roared. "I don't care if Birnam Wood has come to Dunsinane. No man can kill me. Open the gates!"

The battle was fierce. But within minutes, Malcolm's soldiers had taken the castle. Everywhere, men lay dying.

Macduff crept down a corridor, hunting for Macbeth.

Macduff spun and saw Macbeth, his eyes blazing and his sword dripping with blood.

"You can't kill me," sneered Macbeth. "No one born of a woman can hurt me."

"Then prepare to die, you murderer," said Macduff grimly. "For I was never born! I was cut from my mother's dead body."

Macbeth threw back his head and laughed. "So, the witches tricked me," he snarled. "Very well. At least I'll die fighting!" And he ran at Macduff.

The two men fought like demons.
Their swords flashed through the
air, and clashed against
each other.

Then all at once, Macbeth slipped. He reached out to steady himself, but it was too late. Macduff's sword was raised, ready to strike.

In a moment the blade came slicing down, and it was all over.

"Hail Malcolm, King of Scotland," Macduff panted.

Macbeth lay dead on the ground, where his greed for power had brought him. His bloody deeds had led to the bloodiest of ends.

William Shakespeare
1564-1616

William Shakespeare was
born in Stratford-upon-Avon,
England, and became famous
as an actor and writer when he moved to
London. He wrote many poems and almost forty
plays which are still performed and enjoyed today.

Internet links

You can find out more about Shakespeare by going to the
Usborne Quicklinks Website at www.usborne-quicklinks.com
and typing in the keywords 'yr shakespeare'.
Please note that Usborne Publishing cannot be responsible
for the content of any website other than its own.

Designed by Michelle Lawrence

Series designer: Russell Punter

Series editor: Lesley Sims

First published in 2008 by Usborne Publishing Ltd., Usborne House,
83-85 Saffron Hill, London EC1N 8RT, England. www.usborne.com
Copyright © 2008 Usborne Publishing Ltd.